Hawaii's Keiki Christmas COLLECTION

ISLAND HERITAGE

CONTENTS

4 *Keola and the Christmas Pig*
Written by **Marjorie Cochrane**

Keola loves the pig that his father is raising for their Christmas dinner and tries to figure out how to keep it as a pet.

13 *Lisa Li's Christmas Lei*
Written by **Zola Brown**

Lisa Li wants to make the best lei for the Christmas lei contest . . .

26 *The Gecko Who Was Scared of Ceilings*
Written by **Dorothy J. Saurer**

A rhyming story about a gecko who writes Santa Claus for help with his big problem – he's scared to walk on the ceiling like other geckos!

33 *The Legend of the Menehune Santa*
Written by **Larry Rivera**

A tale of old about a sick child, a bright star in
the sky, and an ancient white-bearded Menehune.

38 *The Gift*
Written by **Tandy Newsome**

Alika misses his grandpa who always took him fishing
. . . but then a special gift from the ocean makes Alika's
Christmas one he won't forget.

47 *Cat Heaven*
Written by **Clemi McLaren**

His family is having a difficult time, and Jamie
wants the one thing for Christmas that he
knows he cannot get . . . his cat Nui.

 Illustrations by **Jeff Pagay**

KEOLA AND THE CHRISTMAS PIG
BY MARJORIE COCHRANE

One day when the ocean was spring blue and the coffee trees were covered with blossoms as white as the waves, Keola's father brought home a young pig in the back of his pickup.

"Come, Keola," he called. "Help me mend the fence for a pen for our Christmas pig."

Keola came running. He was puzzled. It was not yet Easter. Why was this a Christmas pig?

"The pig is small now," Keola's father said. "But by December it will be just the right size for our Christmas luau."

Keola was still puzzled. When his father planned such a feast, he and Keola's uncles went hunting in the ohia forest for a wild pig. Why did they need to raise a kalua pig, as a pig baked in the oven is called, on their farm?

Sometimes, his father told him, they could find a fat young pig in the forest. Sometimes the wild pigs were stringy and tough. He looked at Keola thoughtfully.

"And sometimes," he said, "I worry about the forest and the damage that the wild pigs do. Perhaps we should remove the wild pigs from the forests so that the plants they destroy will have a chance to grow again. Then the birds that feed on these plants will return. Perhaps when you are a man, there won't be pigs to hunt. So you will need to know how to raise them."

Keola was not sure he understood, but he loved the taste of kalua pig when the stones of the earthen imu were lifted and the meat, crisp on the outside, juicy inside, was piled on ti-leaves. He was happy, too, to have a small pig to help care for.

"What will we call the pig, Papa?" he asked after the fence was mended and his father had carried the piglet from the pickup to her new home.

"This pig will not have a name," his father said. "This is the pig we will feast on at Christmas time. It is not a pet. If you give this pig a name, you will not want it to be a pig for a luau."

Keola hopped on his bike and rode around and around the farmyard where he could watch the little pig. His cousins had given him the bicycle when they outgrew it. Now it was too small for Keola, too, and rusty as well. He had to turn his knees out to the sides to pedal it because his legs were too long.

"I need a new bike," Keola complained to the pig as he rode past, " A bigger bike. A silver and black bike."

The pig was white and friendly. All that spring when Keola brought food for her and filled her trough with water, she ran to the gate of the pen to meet him. She grunted happily and rubbed her soft wet snout on his bare legs. Keola loved the little pig. And one day when he was sitting in the pen tickling her ears, he whispered to her, "I am going to call you Mauna Kea."

He explained to the piglet that Mauna Kea meant "white mountain." It was also the name of the most splendid mountain on the Big Island of Hawaii where Keola's family grew coffee. Sometimes in the winter they could see snow on top of the mountain and that was why it was called Mauna Kea.

"You are not a mountain," Keola told the pig, "but you are as beautiful and white as the snow and you will grow into a splendid big pig."

When the days turned steamy and the ocean was a flat summer-blue, Mauna Kea grew larger. Keola took her special treats that he gathered in the orchard — avocados which made her short white hair even shinier and sweet mangos and macadamia nuts which she crunched with her strong white teeth.

His father was pleased. "You are doing a fine job raising a pig," he told Keola. "She will be the best kalua pig we have ever had."

When the ocean was deep autumn blue, flecked with white caps, and when the coffee cherries were scarlet and ready to pick, Keola continued to feed and water Mauna Kea each day. But often now there was a lump in his throat when she ran happily to meet him. He wished that she were not so glossy and fat. He wished she were not growing so big. He did not want Mauna Kea to be a kalua pig.

In early December, when the night breezes blowing down the mountain slopes were cold and the daytime winds from the ocean were fair and warm, Keola's mother asked him what he would like for Christmas. He thought a moment and said, "I would like turkey instead of pork for our Christmas luau."

His mother said, "But we have a fine pig nearly ready for Christmas. "And we had a fine turkey for Thanksgiving."

"Turkey is better," said Keola. "Turkey is all I want for Christmas."

This was not entirely true. Keola hopped on the bike and rode across the farmyard to Mauna Kea's pen.

"Mauna Kea," he said to the pig. "What am I to do? I really did hope for a new bicycle for Christmas. A black and silver bike. I want a bike much more than I want turkey. I said I wanted turkey only to keep you safe."

The pig snuffled and looked pleased. Keola's mother came looking for him.

"Hop in the pickup, Keola," she said. "The Christmas tree barge has come. You can help pick out a tree."

The parking lot at the market was full of evergreens. "Where did they come from?" Keola asked his mother.

"From the mainland," she said. "From farms in Oregon and Washington where they grow trees just for Christmas."

The trees did not look much like the evergreens that grew in Hawaii. And while Hawaiian evergreens had little scent, the special scent of these trees filled the parking lot. Keola sniffed their spicy needles. He chose the fattest, spiciest fir tree he could find. They took it home and strung it with bright lights and tinsel and colored balls.

When Keola took food and water to Mauna Kea, he told her about the tree.

"I wish you could see it," he said. "And I wish you could see the Christmas parade tonight. You would love the parade."

Mauna Kea snuffled as though she agreed with Keola.

The parade was exciting. The high school band led the way. Hula dancers followed it. Paniolos (Hawaiian cowboys) rode horses who had floral leis around their necks. A flat bed truck carried a giant whale made of white plumeria blossoms. The queen and her princesses rode past, blowing kisses. Last of all came a fire engine sounding its siren . . . and on the fire engine was Santa himself. Santa threw handfuls of candy to the children watching the parade. Keola scrambled for the candy.

"Look!" he exclaimed, running back to his parents. "Peppermints!" He gave one of the hard candies to his mother and one to his father. He unwrapped one to suck in his own mouth, and he put one in his pocket.

Just before bedtime, he slipped out of the house into the warm star-filled dark. He climbed into Mauna Kea's pen and unwrapped the last peppermint.

"I brought you a treat," he said. "I loved the parade. But I love you best, Mauna Kea."

Early the next morning Keola heard his father calling loudly.

"Keola! Keola! The pig is missing!"

Keola ran to the pen. His father showed him where Mauna Kea had jumped the fence.

"I didn't think she could jump so high," Keola said. He was astonished.

"We must find her," said his father. "I'll drive the pickup down the road to look for her. I want you to hunt for her in the orchard."

Keola went looking. He did not look under the swooping branches of the mango tree because he was afraid he would find her there. He did not look in the grove of macadamia nuts because he was afraid he would find her there. Instead he looked through the coffee orchard because he did not think that was where she would be. If he could not find her, she would be safe.

But on the edge of the orchard, where his father's land joined the ohia forest, stood an avocado tree . . . and under the tree eating avocados was Mauna Kea. She oinked and snuffled and ran to him. Keola put his arms around her and sobbed.

"Run away, Mauna Kea," he said. "Run where I can't find you."

But if she ran into the ohia forest, hunters might shoot her. If he took her back to the pen — he did not want to think about that, either. The only way he could save Mauna Kea was to hide her himself.

He tied the rope he was carrying around her neck and led her under the branches of the mango tree where he did not think anyone would see her. When no one was looking, he carried food and water to her.

His father came back from the search. He was angry. "All that work to raise a pig for our luau," he said, "and now we won't have one after all."

He asked Keola's mother what she thought they should do.

"I think," said Keola's mother, "that we should have turkey for the Christmas feast."

And that very day when she went to the market she bought the largest turkey she could find.

Keola should have been happy. But he was even sadder than before. He knew it was wrong to hide Mauna Kea.

"Why do you look so sad?" his father said to him at dinner time. "Is it because the pig is gone?"

Keola nodded.

"I know you love kalua pig," his father said. "I love it, too." And he sighed and looked as sad as Keola.

Keola burst into tears.

"I know where our pig is," he cried. "But papa, I love her like she is. I don't want her for our luau. I want her in her pen for Christmas."

Then he cried harder. "And I really, really want a new bicycle, too."

Keola's father looked puzzled. Then he looked angry. Then he sighed a second time.

"Too late for this year's luau anyway," he said finally. "We now have a turkey for Christmas. And who knows, perhaps you will find a big surprise under the Christmas tree. But," he added sternly, "you should not have hidden the pig."

"Her name is Mauna Kea," Keola said.

His father sighed a third time.

"What we will do is this," he decided after he had thought a while. "We will use your Mauna Kea to produce piglets. Then we will be sure to have pigs for our luaus. And none of those pigs," he said even more sternly, "will have names."

But Keola was not listening. Already he was thinking that the first piglet would be named Mauna Loa, "the long mountain," and the next one would be named Mele Kalikimaka, which means "Merry Christmas," and the next one...

PAU

12

Lisa Li's Christmas Lei

By Zola Brown

Lisa Li came bouncing into the living room after school. She was a perky second grader with a round, happy face.

She dropped her backpack on the floor and ran into the kitchen where her mother was fixing her snack. Lisa Li sat down and quickly reached for the carrot sticks and cookies her mother had placed on the table.

"Guess what, Mom?" she said. "Our class is having a contest. We're making lei for Christmas. There's going to be a prize for the prettiest, the funniest, and the most original — that means sort of different—and then we will get to give our lei to someone we like. Will you help me?"

"Well," her mother hedged, "What sort of help am I supposed to give?"

"You could maybe help me get an idea. Or help me thread needles. Or pick flowers. That kind of stuff," replied Lisa Li.

"Flower lei are nice," suggested her mother, Mrs. Kumaki. "Our yard has several different kinds. You can go out after your snack and pick some."

Lisa Li finished her last cookie and carrot stick, finished the juice in her glass, and slid off the chair. Then she took a plastic grocery bag from the drawer under the sink and went outside.

The first flowers she saw were the yellow-centered white plumeria on the small trees that lined the driveway. She quickly filled her bag with the fragrant flowers.

When she went inside, her mother was waiting with a lei needle threaded with a yard of kite string. It didn't take Lisa Li long to sew the flowers into a pretty, sweet scented lei.

"Mom," Lisa Li called to Mrs. Kumaki, "Do you have some ribbon? I'd like a little bow for my lei."

Mrs. Kumaki got out her sewing box and found a bit of pink ribbon — Lisa Li's favorite color. She made the bow and tied it onto the pretty lei.

"Isn't it a bit early to take tomorrow, if the contest is on Friday?" she asked Lisa Li.

"Miss Levi will put them in the refrigerator," confided Lisa Li. "She said she will take care of the perishable ones — she meant the ones that wouldn't keep well."

The lei was put into a clear plastic cake container and stored in the refrigerator.

The next morning Lisa Li was impatient to start to school. She hurriedly got ready and ate her breakfast without dawdling. Carrying the lei very carefully, she began the six-block long walk to school.

She had to pass several houses in the first and second blocks. Then came a vacant lot, then several more residences, and the last blocks before the school were stores and shops.

As she passed Mrs. Dugan's house in the next block, she saw Mrs. Dugan step out onto her lanai to pick up the newspaper. Mrs. Dugan sometimes stayed with Lisa Li if her mother couldn't be home in the afternoon.

"Good morning!" called Lisa Li. "How are you today?" Then she noticed Mrs. Dugan's sad face. "Is something the matter?"

16

"Puppy died yesterday," said the old woman with tears in her eyes. Puppy was Mrs. Dugan's dog. He was an old dog, really, but he had always been called "Puppy."

Lisa Li hesitated just a bit. Then, opening her plastic container, she slowly took out her beautiful plumeria lei. Putting it around Mrs. Dugan's neck, she kissed her and gave her a hug. "I'm really sorry," she said softly in Mrs. Dugan's ear. "I loved Puppy, too."

At school, several of the second graders had made lei. There was a white and yellow plumeria one just like Lisa Li's except it had a green ribbon. There were other plumeria lei, one made out of toy cars and trucks, one made from drinking straws cut into pieces, and one made from dollar bills folded to look like roses.

The day seemed to go quickly, but Lisa Li could hardly keep her mind on her lessons. What she was thinking about was lei, lei, lei.

At home, after school, she sat and ate her snack and thought about her lei some more.

"Mom, is it okay if I take the pennies out of my money jar? I have another idea for a lei," Lisa Li said.

"Are you going to enter more than one lei?" asked her mother, "You already made one."

"No, Mom, but something happened to the one I made yesterday. May I have some see-through wrap and some crinkly red ribbons?"

Her mother got out a box of green plastic food wrap and a small roll of Christmas ribbon and handed them to Lisa Li.

Lisa Li carefully made bundles of twenty pennies, rolled them in the wrap, and then tied the little bundles together with the red ribbon. When she was finished, she called, "Will you please come and make the ends curly?"

The finished lei was pretty but a bit heavy. Lisa Li thought it had 400 pennies in it. She set it beside her book bag so that she wouldn't forget it.

The next day, Wednesday, Lisa Li was impatient to start to school with her pretty, unusual lei. She skipped along the street until she was within two blocks of school. Then she heard something. It sounded like a bell ringing! Soon she saw that it really was a bell. A lady standing beside a kettle was ringing it. A sign on the kettle said, "Help give the poor a Christmas dinner."

Lisa Li thought about poor kids she had heard about who were not as lucky as she. She would have a good dinner with ham, turkey, or perhaps roasted duck and the other little kids might not have even a peanut butter sandwich. (Lisa Li did not like peanut butter; she liked rice and Spam.)

Slowly she took her pretty penny lei out of her bag. She draped it over the kettle and ran quickly down the street. The lady called after her, "Mahalo! Thank you so much! Have a happy day!"

More children had brought their lei to school. One was made of dendrobium orchids. Lisa Li called them "baby orchids." There were more plumeria lei tied with different colored ribbons. One plumeria was a double one which looked as full as a carnation one. Lisa Li really liked it. She thought it was the prettiest. Someone else had made one with pennies. Another was made from lacy-looking leaves, only the veins remaining after the tender green part of the leaf was eaten by insects.

"Mom, will you help me again? I need to make another lei," said Lisa Li when she came home after school.

Mrs. Kumaki's curiosity had been aroused regarding the missing lei, but she knew Lisa Li would tell her, if she wanted to.

"What are you going to make this time?" Mrs. Kumaki asked.

"Well, I've made pretty and original," Lisa Li said. "I think I will make funny this time. May I have some of Mouse's food?" (Mouse was the tiny gray and white kitten that had strayed into their yard one day. Not finding her owner, they had kept her and named her "Mouse.")

"Of course," replied Mrs. Kumaki and she went to get a bowlful of the tiny, multi-colored donut-shaped bits.

Lisa Li quickly strung the little circles. "I think some brown ribbon would be nice for this. Do you have any?"

Mrs. Kumaki remembered that she had some ribbon left over after stringing some kukui nut lei. There was just enough to make a little bow.

It was a damp morning so Lisa Li wore her red boots and yellow poncho on Thursday. As she was passing the vacant lot, she saw some birds hungrily picking at the ground where someone had dropped a hamburger wrapper with a bit of bun stuck to it. The birds flew up at her presence, but when she stood quietly, they fluttered back to peck at the tiny portion of food.

She watched them thoughtfully for a moment and then hung the cat food lei on a tall bush. Almost immediately, a bird flew over and began pecking at a circle. Other birds joined the first and the lei began to fall to bits. Lisa Li smiled and ran the rest of the way to school.

By now, most of the second graders had their lei made. Only Lisa Li and two others had not brought theirs.

"Children," Miss Levi reminded them, "Tomorrow, Friday, is the last day to bring your lei to class. Remember, the principal and two of the other teachers will be the judges. Also remember you may invite your friends and neighbors, as well as your parents. You may give your lei to a friend during our program."

By now, Lisa Li was out of ideas . . . Her feet lagged on the way home. Just one more chance!

There had been so many different kinds of lei turned in so far, twenty-five or twenty-six, she thought. Some were funny—George's was made out of plastic people. Some were lovely, made out of fresh flowers and silky ribbons. There were the original ones made from odd materials, such as the Styrofoam packing-curl lei made by Sandy.

She sat at the table disconsolately, munching on sugar cookies and sipping milk as she thought. All at once, an idea popped into her head!

"Mom, is it all right if I make cookies for dessert tonight?" she asked.

"That's a great idea," answered her mother. "I have an easy chocolate chip cookie recipe one of my friends gave me. I'll help you get the ingredients together."

She got the sugar, flour, butter, chocolate chips, vanilla, and the other ingredients that were needed, together with a big bowl and spoon. Then Lisa Li sprayed the cookie sheets. She poured, sifted, stirred and blended until all the ingredients were mixed together. Then she took a spoonful of dough and flattened it out on the cookie sheet.

"You don't have to do that," said her mother.

"Yes, I do," contradicted Lisa Li. Then she found the donut cutter and slipped the small circle cutter out of the larger cutter. After she had flattened a sheet full of cookies, she carefully cut a tiny circle out of the center of each one.

When the oven was hot and all the cookies were ready, her mother opened the oven door and slipped them in.

Lisa Li sat and watched the clock for the ten minutes required to bake the cookies. Then Mrs. Kumaki took them out and set them to cool. Finally, they were cool enough to remove from the cookie sheets.

May I have some red ribbon and some clear plastic wrap?" asked Lisa Li.

When her mother brought them, Lisa Li began wrapping each cookie separately.

Then she threaded the ribbon through the eye of a large darning needle. Carefully she strung the cookies on the ribbon, tying a knot between the cookies. When she had 31 cookies on her lei, she tied the ends of the ribbon together and added a big bow of red ribbon. Then she made a second lei like the first one, but with a few more cookies on it. When she was done, there were 10 cookies left on the plate.

"That's for dessert," she told her mother.

At school the next afternoon, the lei were displayed neatly on a table. The ribbons for the prettiest, funniest, and most original were on the three chosen leis. Miss Levi had

made 30 carnation lei. She had tied pink ribbons on the girls' lei and blue on the boys' lei. The boys' flowers were white carnations which had a blue edge; the girls' flowers had a pink edge. She presented them to each child with a hug.

Just before the awards were given, Miss Levi announced: "This year we are giving a special award — one for the MOST DELICIOUS LEI!" She held up Lisa Li's two cookie lei. "Lisa Li wants to share her lei with EVERYONE!"

Miss Levi clipped the ribbons of the lei with a pair of scissors and slid the cookies onto a large plate. She put a blue "Special Award" ribbon beside the plate of cookies.

That afternoon, when Lisa Li and her mother walked home after the prgram, Lisa Li sighed with happiness.

"You know, Mom," she said, "I was glad to get a ribbon, but what made me happiest was the fun I had making and sharing all the lei."

Then she told her mother what had happened to the first three lei.

Pau

MRS. KUMAKI'S CHOCOLATE CHIP COOKIES

1 cup sugar

1 cup brown sugar, packed
 (light or dark brown)

2/3 cup butter (or margarine)

2/3 cup butter-flavored Crisco

3 teaspoons vanilla

3 small or medium eggs

3 1/2 cups flour

1 teaspoon baking soda

1 teaspoon salt

1 cup chopped walnuts

1 12-ounce package chocolate chips

1 cup coconut (shredded or flaked)

Turn on oven to 375 degrees. Mix sugars, butter, Crisco, vanilla, and eggs in a large bowl, stirring with a wooden spoon. Sift flour, baking soda and salt together and stir into mix. Stir in nuts, then add chocolate chips, and then add the coconut.

(Coconut may be omitted, if desired.)

(For chocolate-y cookies, 1/3 cup of cocoa powder may be added; if this makes the mix too dry, add 1 more small egg.)

Drop by teaspoon onto greased cookie sheet.

Bake for 8 to 10 minutes.

Cool slightly and remove from cookie sheet with spatula.

Makes about 75 cookies — More if you remove the centers as Lisa Li did!

THE GECKO

WHO WAS SCARED OF CEILINGS

BY DOROTHY J. SAURER

Gary the gecko was cute as could be
But he had a big problem, because you see
He always got a HORRIBLE feeling
When it came time to walk on the ceiling!
The thought of it just made him sick,
He knew, he KNEW that his feet wouldn't stick...
His parents just couldn't understand
"Just walk like all geckos!" they'd demand.
"Fish all swim and birds all fly
And GECKOS all walk way up high!"
On and on, they'd scold and fuss...
"Floors are for humans, ceilings, for US!
Each foot is like a suction cup
And that is what will hold you up..."

His family coaxed, pleaded and dared him,
But the more they talked, the more they scared him.
His brothers thought that he was faking
Until they saw how he was shaking.
His auntie, lively as could be,
Said, "Watch ceiling aerobics on TV!"
But, with each suggestion Gary cried
And ran off to a corner to hide.
His classmates called him 'fraidy cat
And other awful names like that
They teased him and made him squirm
When saying he should have been a worm.

The doctors had no cure or healing
For a gecko who was scared of the ceiling.
One old, old gecko, known to be wise,
Told Gary, "Just close your eyes...
You won't have a scared feeling
When you can't SEE you're on the ceiling."
His brother thought it would be neat
If he just put gum on all his feet!
A shoemaker made him boots with spikes,
Just the thing for ceiling hikes.
But Gary wouldn't try them on...
One look at spikes and he was gone!
His great grandpa, not much of a talker,
Offered to let him use his walker.
But Gary just ignored them all
And still was scared that he would fall.

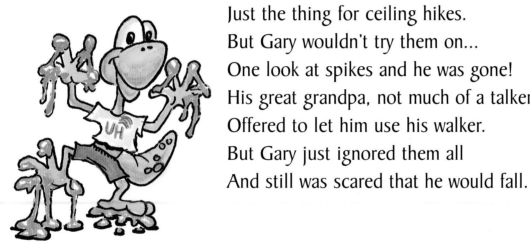

Then Christmas came and Gary wrote
Santa Claus a special note:
"Dear Santa, I don't want toys
Like other gecko girls and boys.
I just want something to help me
Be braver than I seem to be.
I don't know WHAT you could bring—
No one else has anything . . ."

When Gary awoke on Christmas morn,
He felt so sad and forlorn,
But OH!   A package was under the tree
What was it??? He couldn't wait to see!
He tore open the wrappings and found
Something very soft and round,
Made by "Elf No. 53".
What was it? Well, you see...

It wasn't a sticky shoe or boot,
It was a TUMMY PARACHUTE!
He quickly strapped it
　　　on his tummy
And knew he didn't need
　　　anything gummy.

He climbed the wall
　　　with a confident feeling
And without stopping,
　　　STEPPED ONTO THE CEILING!

He knew the 'chute would open
　　　if he fell,
So he crossed without a moan
　　　or yell.
Then he turned and walked back again,
　　　Twice, 3 times, 6, then 10!

With a huge, huge grin and a loud hoot,
He pushed the button of the parachute.
Down he fell, there was a POP,
The chute opened for a smooth drop.
All his brothers wanted to try
To float down from the ceiling so high!
And Gary let them each have a turn,
And watching, what do you think he learned?
He knew, with the most wondrous feeling

HE NO LONGER WAS SCARED TO WALK ON THE CEILING!

The Legend of the Menehune Santa

By Larry Rivera

One warm Hawaiian night, many times ago, a keiki tossed and turned in his bed. His mother, the daughter of the King of Kauai, summoned a great Kahuna, as she was afraid for her son.

"He is sick," she said, "The Great God Haloma must be angry. Our house is in shame!" The powerful Kahuna consoled the woman and began many incantations in an attempt to break the spell of sickness from the child.

Far above in the mountains, a place where it rains called Mt. Waialeale, lived the "little people" of Kauai called the Menehunes. The Menehunes had remarkable strength, loud voices that could be heard on Oahu during times of celebration and also possessed great energy and capacity for work. It was their custom never to be seen and they would leave a job incomplete if ever observed by a native.

They were annoyed by the Kahuna's noise-making and soon sent an emissary to Wailua where the pounding originated. Because of great energy, he was quickly there and from a clever hiding place discovered the source of the trouble.

His return to the rain mountain signaled for an immediate council of leaders who determined that special potions made from leaves brought by the Bird God Kano should be given to the child. That night, the Menehunes silently came down from the mountains to Wailua. They administered the medicines and awaited the recovery.

But the child was no better.

The Menehunes were perplexed! As all-powerful as they were, the sickness stymied them! Suddenly, down from the inner recesses of the mountains came the Old One, the ancient white bearded Menehune who was the supreme ruler of the "little people."

"Your efforts will do you no good," he explained. "The child will not be cured until a greater homage is paid! Look toward the sky!"

The Menehunes lifted their faces and in the heavens perceived a bright new star.
Its light was all-powerful.

"Pray to the star," the white bearded leader commanded, "Your wishes will be heard."

The "little people" flattened themselves against the earth.

Suddenly, the child stirred, the sickness leaving him and the Menehunes slipped away . . . as the mother returned to his side.

Another mother saw a Son that day, she for the first time. He was in a manger.

PAU

Since the time of the missionaries, our Hawaiians have always had a charming way of appropriating the Bible stories and tying them in, without distortion, to their own ancient legends of gods and powers beyond the sight of man. In his enchanting *Legend of the Menehune Santa*, Larry Rivera is also telling the Bethlehem story through the compelling power of that new bright star seen in the heavens the night when Christ was born. He casts his lei of song back some 1900 years to unite our fabled "little people" of Kauai with the major happening on the other side of the earth on that first Christmas Eve. Fresh and poetic, this is the Hawaiian way of telling the imperishable story.

Kathryn Hulme, Author - The Nun's Story

THE GIFT

By Tandy Newsome

On an island called Hawaii, on the rocky slope of a volcano, lived a young boy named Alika. He lived down the road from his grandpa, who was his favorite person in all the world. The old man was Hawaiian and spent his days fishing in all the same places his grandpa had taken him fishing when he was a boy. He knew how to make fish hooks out of bone, fishing poles out of bamboo, and a good time out of nothing at all. He loved to tell tales about old Hawaii, and had a small collection of old Hawaiian implements, most of which had been in his family over the years. But one such item, unquestionably his favorite, was an ancient Hawaiian fish hook carved out of bone, which he had found at one of his special fishing spots. He wore it proudly on a braided cord around his neck. He once told Alika that, finding it as he did, he considered it a gift from a fellow fisherman, and that made it very special to him.

"Funny thing about gifts," he had said, "Really special ones have a way of being given over and over again." Alika had admired the polished hook many times and sometimes wondered about the Hawaiian fisherman who had carved it.

Every Saturday, when Alika had no school, he woke up very early and anxiously waited for the familiar sound of his Grandpa's rattly, old truck, bumbling down the road. And when the flash of the headlights flickered past his window, he would quickly pull the covers up so only his eyes could peek out. The boy would pretend to be asleep, and his grandpa would pretend to shake him awake, until they were both rolling on the bed with laughter. Then Grandpa would make his usual announcement.

"Fish are early risers, and you have to get up extra early if you want to surprise them!"

Alika would eagerly climb out of bed and jump into his clothes. His grandpa had already packed a lunch of musubi, icy lemonade, and shiny, red mountain apples from the tree in his backyard. Then Alika would grab his pole, they'd climb into Grandpa's old blue pickup, and off they'd go.

Down through the tall koa forests they'd drive. Sometimes they were lucky enough to catch a glimpse of the Hawaiian hawk who lived at the edge of the woods. Winding between the cane fields, they could hardly wait for that first, shimmering sparkle of the rising sun on the blue Pacific Ocean. Alika would look over at his grandpa, his face beaming with a smile. They didn't have to say anything at all. They both loved Saturdays.

As they neared the coast, they passed the colorful patchwork of homes, made with plastic tarps and blankets, all tied together like a circus tent. Their loose ends flapped in the breeze making a funny popping sound. Grandpa had explained to his grandson that many of the people of their island didn't have homes of their own, and some of them had chosen to live together down by the beach. One particular man they had seen many times. His red-flowered shirt and palm-leaf hat had become a welcome sight at the end of the beach road. His many years of living outside in the hot, tropical sun had turned his skin into soft brown leather. And though he was always busy weaving hats from the leaves of the coconut palm, they could always count on his friendly wave and smile.

"I would love living at the beach all the time, Grandpa," Alika had said. "We could go fishing and swimming every day."

"Yes, it would be fun for a while, Alika, but at the end of the day, when the sun goes down, it's nice to have a place of your very own to go home to. You and I have such a place, and these people have none."

There had been a sad, faraway sound in his voice that made Alika feel sorry for the palm-hat man and the rest of the homeless people. His grandpa had looked over at him with a gentle smile.

"I am very lucky to have someone like you to go fishing with, and a place to go home to at the end of the day." Alika felt very lucky, too.

They would spend the day fishing, picking opihi, and gathering seaweed. They shared their lunch under the shade of a huge mango tree, always saving a little for the family of mongooses who lived in the ginger patch nearby. And when the last golden ray of sun lit the surface of the ocean, they silently, but happily, got into the truck to go home. Grandpa always left most of the fish with the people who lived in the tents. He liked to help people whenever he had the chance.

They spent many Saturdays at their favorite fishing spot by the sea, but as Alika continued to grow bigger and stronger, his grandpa seemed to grow smaller and weaker. Their fishing days became shorter, because the old man would get really tired by the middle of the day. Alika had begun to carry all the fishing poles and bait, and would sometimes have to help his grandpa get back to the truck.

One day while Alika was at school, his grandpa went fishing as usual, but did not come home at the end of the day. It was not clear exactly what happened to him, because his body was never found, but his pole and unopened lunch were left on the rocky shore, and it was believed by most that he fell into the ocean and drowned. Alika could not eat or sleep for many days after that. He no longer wanted to see the ocean. His fishing pole stood in the corner of his room, collecting dust. His heart ached so deeply, he felt that his life could never be happy again.

Months passed and Alika tried to keep his mind busy with his schoolwork and household chores, but as the Christmas holidays drew near, he could not stop thinking about his grandpa and he wondered what had happened to him. He still missed him deeply and always felt somehow that he was nearby. But he still could not bring himself to go to the ocean. The night before Christmas he went to bed remembering the last Christmas morning he and his grandpa had shared. They had gotten up extra early to go fishing so they could surprise the family with the gift of a wonderful fish dinner. He drifted off to sleep with the happy memories of that day.

Early Christmas morning he was awakened just as the sun was coming up by the sound of an old truck coming down the road. Still half asleep, he staggered out of bed, expecting his grandpa to burst into his room at any moment, ready to go fishing, just as he had done so many times before. Looking out his window, he thought he saw an old blue truck bouncing down the dusty cane road. He rubbed his eyes to be sure he was really awake, and then ran out to jump on his bike. His feet flew to the pedals and his bike flew down the road.

"Grandpa!" he called out hopefully, but the truck was soon out of sight, leaving a cloud of billowing dust behind. He hurried down the winding road to the beach, the colorful tents now a blurry rainbow, as seen through his watery eyes.

When he made his way to the end of the road, there was a crowd of people standing at the water's edge. Between them he could see the figure of the man in the red-flowered shirt. He was lying on the sand, soaking wet and shaking, trying desperately to catch his breath. His eyes widened as he told how he had slipped off the rocks into the water, had struggled helplessly against the surf, and had called and called for help.

"And just when I felt myself slipping beneath the waves, something came out of nowhere," he gasped, " to lift me out of the water and gently toss me ashore. It felt like the mighty hand of the ocean itself." Having told his miraculous tale, he collapsed in a tired heap on the sand, thankful for his good fortune.

It was only then that Alika remembered what had brought him down to the beach in the first place. His eyes searched the dusty road one last time for the old blue truck. Seeing nothing, he turned to go. The man in the red-flowered shirt nudged his arm and spoke, more calmly now than before.

"You didn't come all the way down to the ocean just to turn and go, did you? Before I slipped off those rocks, I was going to fish all morning so that all of my friends could share a fish dinner for Christmas. Now it is late already, and I have caught nothing." He looked knowingly at Alika and said, "I know you are a good fisherman." All at once there came an unexpected gust of wind which sprayed Alike with a fine ocean mist. When the cold drops of sea water hit his face, he realized how much he had missed coming to the ocean. Being there in the warm morning sun, the salty breeze brought with it a flood of wonderful memories of good times spent with his grandpa, times that had been hard to think about for many months. The breeze left as suddenly as it had come and seemed to take much of Alika's grief and sadness away with it.

He quickly offered to go fishing with the palm-hat man for the rest of the day. They caught enough fish for a grand Christmas feast, and while they fished, they got to know each other. Sam, as he called himself, taught Alika to make small fish out of the palm leaves, and the tricky way to make a quick hat. He told him stories about his life, and he shared his lunch with the boy under a familiar mango tree. Alika told Sam about his grandpa and what a good fisherman he was. He shared some of Grandpa's best Hawaiian tales.

When it was time for Alika to go home, Sam reached into his pocket, which was still damp from the morning's excitement.

"I found this around my neck after being tossed ashore this morning. I don't know where it came from. It seemed to be a gift from the ocean to me, and now I would like to give it to you."

In his hand was Grandpa's braided cord with the carved bone fish hook on it. Sam put it around Alika's neck.

"Merry Christmas," he said, "And by the way, next Saturday, please get up earlier. You have to get up really early if you want to surprise the fish."

And Alika did.

PAU

CAT HEAVEN

By Clemi McLaren

Jamie glanced up to find the eagle eye of his new teacher fixed on him.

"Jamie Gomes," Mrs. Yamada said crisply, and she pointed her bony finger at the assignment on the board. "Write a letter to Santa Claus about the one thing you want most for Christmas."

Jamie sighed and looked down at his crumpled paper. "Dear Santa," his letter began. "I want one thing, but you cannot get." His friend Sean said there was no Santa Claus, that your parents bought all the stuff and toy companies made a lot of money.

Dear Santa,

I want one thing, but you cannot get.
The one thing I want is my cat Nui. We wen take her to the pound on Monday. My mom says for sure somebody going come along and adopt one smart cat like Nui, but my friend Sean say no way. He say they kill the cats in one small gas chamber he seen on TV news. Not enough people looking for adopt one cat, thas why.

This one bad year, Santa. My parents getting one divorce, jus li dat. Dad working on Maui now. Has one girlfriend over there. So last week, my brother, my mom and me, we move to one small apartment. Cat too much humbug, mom says. And she no want trouble with The Land Lord. So, we take Nui to the pound. My brother Mark wants power rangers, my mom wants a night sleep. I just want Nui.

Hey, never mind power rangers. My bradda probly wants Nui more better.

He picked up his pencil and wrote.

"The one thing I want is my cat Nui. We wen take her to the pound on Monday. My mom says for sure somebody going come along and adopt one smart cat like Nui, but my friend Sean say no way. He say they kill the cats in one small gas chamber he seen on TV news. Not enough people looking for adopt one cat, thas why."

Mrs. Yamada was still watching him. Jamie missed his old school and his old teacher, who used to play ukulele after lunch while they sat on the carpet and sang. His dad always picked him up after A-plus. Some days he took Jamie and his brother fishing.

"This one bad year, Santa. My parents getting one divorce, jus li dat. Dad working on Maui now. Has one girlfriend over there. So last week, my brother, my mom and me, we move to one small apartment. Cat too much humbug, mom says. And she no want trouble with The Land Lord. So, we take Nui to the pound. My brother Mark wants power rangers, my mom wants a night sleep. I just want Nui."

"Hey, never mind power rangers. My bradda probly wants Nui more better."

The final bell rang.

"Put your letters in the tray," Mrs. Yamada yelled above the scuffle of books and bodies. "I'll correct spelling, and we'll mail them to Santa tomorrow. Just in time for Christmas!"

Jamie skimmed his letter, shook his head, and threw it into the waste basket as he dashed out of the room.

Jamie's mom had a chance to work at the hotel Christmas Eve for double pay, leaving Jamie to explain to his 5-year-old brother why they were not going to see their dad.

"Because he getting us for New Year's, like I tole you 60 times already..."

"Why he no come here?"

Jamie shrugged. "They're working things out. And that's how they worked it. You 'tink 'dey ask my opinion? Come on, we go put lights on da tree."

But Mark just shook his head, eyes brimming with tears. "Junk, da tree," he whispered, looking up at the table-top tree Jamie had just assembled by sticking some skinny branches into a plastic base.

"Dis whole place is junk," Mark sobbed. "And ...I want Nui!"

"Yea, me too," Jamie sat down next to his brother on the floor. Sean said they kept the animals at the pound for two weeks. This was the 14th day since they had dropped Nui off. Would they really put cats to sleep on Christmas Eve?

"Some sleep!" he said under his breath. "No more wake up!"

That night he said a special Christmas prayer. "Dear God, please take good care of Nui in cat heaven."

Jamie fell asleep picturing cat heaven, full of cats basking in sunny window sills and cats chasing mice and then letting them go, because God wouldn't let them bite the heads off like on Earth.

When he heard the faint meow, he thought it was part of his dream. He sat up in bed, listening to the silence. The apartment was dark; his mother must have turned off the TV and gone to bed. He got up and went into the living room. There were lights on the junk tree and presents on the table underneath. But no cat.

Jamie swallowed down his tears, ashamed of himself for wanting so badly to believe in magic. What a baby he was!

And then his mother was standing in the doorway, wearing her pink bathrobe, and in her arms was a large orange tabby cat.

"I couldn't keep this present quiet," she said, smiling.

"Santa didn't get my letter....Besides, there's no such thing."

His mother nodded. "Santa Yamada . . . She found your letter in the trash."

Nui jumped down and rubbed herself against Jamie's legs. His mother came and folded him in her arms.

"I'm sorry, son. I've counted on you so much that I let myself forget you're still a kid. I'm so sorry . . . for everything. And I promise, next year is going to be better."

"Mom, do you think Nui will forgive us?"

But the cat had already moved off and was carefully curling herself into a ball at Mark's feet. She would be the first thing the child would see when he woke up on Christmas morning.

PAU